THE WORLD OF
PETER RABBIT
AND FRIENDS™
BEDTIME
STORY BOOK
VOLUME 2

THE WORLD OF
PETER RABBIT
AND FRIENDS ™
BEDTIME
STORY BOOK
VOLUME 2

From the authorized animated series
based on the original tales by
BEATRIX POTTER

F. WARNE & Co

FREDERICK WARNE

Published by the Penguin Group
Penguin Books Ltd, 27 Wrights Lane, London W8 5TZ, England
Penguin Books USA Inc., 375 Hudson Street, New York, N.Y. 10014, USA
Penguin Books Australia Ltd, Ringwood, Victoria, Australia
Penguin Books Canada Ltd, 10 Alcorn Avenue, Toronto, Ontario, Canada, M4V 3B2
Penguin Books (N.Z.) Ltd, 182-190 Wairau Road, Auckland 10, New Zealand

Penguin Books Ltd, Registered Offices: Harmondsworth, Middlesex, England

This edition first published by Frederick Warne & Co. 1996
1 3 5 7 9 10 8 6 4 2

ISBN 0 7232 4381 6

Manufactured in China by Imago Publishing Limited

CONTENTS

THE TALE OF THE FLOPSY BUNNIES AND MRS TITTLEMOUSE

It is said that the effect of eating too much lettuce is "soporific."
I have never felt sleepy after eating lettuces; but then I am not a rabbit.
They certainly had a very soporific effect upon the Flopsy Bunnies!

When Benjamin Bunny grew up, he married his Cousin Flopsy.
They had a large family, and they were very improvident and cheerful.
I do not remember the separate names of their children; they were
generally called the "Flopsy Bunnies".

As there was not always quite enough to eat, Benjamin used to borrow cabbages from Flopsy's brother, Peter Rabbit, who kept a nursery garden.

Sometimes Peter Rabbit had no cabbages to spare. When this happened, the Flopsy Bunnies went across the field to a rubbish heap, in the ditch outside Mr McGregor's garden.

Mr McGregor's rubbish heap was a mixture. There were jam pots and paper bags, and some rotten vegetable marrows and an old boot or two. One day – oh joy! – there were a quantity of overgrown lettuces.

A little wood-mouse was picking over the rubbish among the jam pots. Her name was Mrs Tittlemouse.

"Good afternoon, Ma'am," said Benjamin Bunny. "Pray excuse my youngsters – they have waited overlong for their lunch today!"

"Then I think I shall go home," said Mrs Tittlemouse, "before I am eaten in mistake for a lettuce!"

Mrs Tittlemouse lived alone in a bank under a hedge. Such a funny house!

There were yards and yards of sandy passages, leading to storerooms and nut and seed cellars.

There was a kitchen, a parlour, a pantry, and a larder. Also, there was Mrs Tittlemouse's bedroom, where she slept in a little box bed!

Mrs Tittlemouse was a most terribly particular little mouse, always sweeping and dusting the soft sandy floors.

Sometimes a beetle lost its way in the passages. "Shuh! shuh! little dirty feet!" said Mrs Tittlemouse, clattering her dust-pan.

And one day a little old woman ran up and down in a red spotty cloak. "Your house is on fire, Mother Ladybird! Fly away home to your children!"

Another day, a big fat spider came in to shelter from the rain. "Beg pardon, is this not Miss Muffet's?" "Go away, you bold bad spider! Leaving ends of cobweb all over my nice clean house!" Mrs Tittlemouse bundled the spider out at a window.

It was dinner time. "I shall go to my furthest storeroom and fetch cherry stones and thistle-down seed..." said Mrs Tittlemouse. Suddenly round a corner, she met Babbitty Bumble. "Zizz, Bizz, Bizz!" said the bumble bee, in a peevish squeak, and she sidled down a side passage.

Three or four other bees buzzed fiercely. "I am not in the habit of letting lodgings; this is an intrusion!" said Mrs Tittlemouse crossly. "I will have them turned out! I wonder who would help me? . . . Mr Benjamin Bunny, of course! Benjamin Bunny will help me drive out these tiresome bees!"

13

Mrs Tittlemouse went back to the rubbish heap.

The Flopsy Bunnies had simply stuffed lettuces and by degrees, one after another, they had been overcome with slumber.

Benjamin was not so much overcome as his children. Before going to sleep he was sufficiently wide awake to put a paper bag over his head to keep off the flies. The little Flopsy Bunnies slept delightfully in the warm sun.

Mrs Tittle-mouse rustled across the paper bag, and awakened Benjamin Bunny.

"Mr Benjamin, I am so sorry to disturb you, but as we are both acquainted with Mr Peter Rabbit I thought to ask a favour of you... oh Mr Benjamin, I am having such trouble with *bees* in my house!"

"Bees, yes, indeed Ma'am, very tiresome creatures," said Benjamin sleepily.

A robin arrived with a whir of wings and a flash of red. "Oh, Mr Red-breast!" said Mrs Tittlemouse, "could *you* help me with my nest of bees?"

Then they heard a heavy tread above their heads. Mr McGregor was approaching. "The Flopsy Bunnies! Mr McGregor is sure to see the Flopsy Bunnies," said Mrs Tittlemouse. "We must wake them up, we must warn them!" But it was impossible to wake the Flopsy Bunnies.

The robin darted around Mr
McGregor's head, trying to distract
him. Suddenly, he emptied out a
sackful of lawn mowings right upon
the top of the sleeping Flopsy Bunnies!
Benjamin shrank down under his paper bag.
Mrs Tittlemouse hid in a jam pot.

The little rabbits smiled sweetly in
their sleep under the shower of
grass. Mr McGregor looked down.
He saw some funny little brown
tips of ears sticking up through
the lawn mowings. He stared
at them for some time.

Presently a fly settled on one of them and it moved. Mr McGregor climbed down on to the rubbish heap – "One, two, three, four! five! six leetle rabbits!" said he as he dropped them into his sack.

Mr McGregor tied up the sack and left it on the wall. He went to put away the mowing machine.

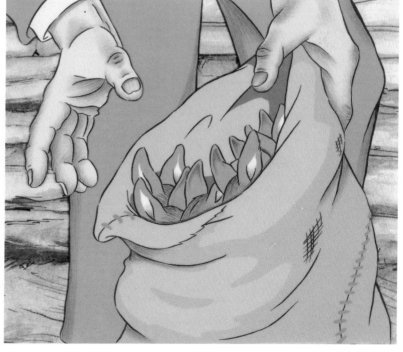

Then Mrs Tittlemouse came out of her jam pot, and Benjamin took the
paper bag off his head. They could see the sack, up on the wall.
Just then Mrs Flopsy Bunny (who had remained at home) came across
the field.

She looked suspiciously at the sack and wondered where everybody was? "Mr McGregor has caught your babies and put them in this sack!" said Mrs Tittlemouse.

Benjamin and Flopsy were in despair; they could not undo the string.

"My poor babies, what shall we do?" said Flopsy. But Mrs Tittlemouse was a resourceful person. "Why, Mrs Tittlemouse, whatever can you be doing?" said Benjamin. She was nibbling a hole in the bottom corner of the sack!

The little rabbits were pulled out and pinched to wake them.

Their parents stuffed the empty
sack with three rotten vegetable
marrows, an old blacking-
brush and two decayed
turnips.

"We'll see what old
McGregor thinks about
that!" said Benjamin, and
they all hid under a bush
and watched for him.
    Mrs Tittlemouse hastily
said goodday and went home.

Mr McGregor had come back to fetch the sack. He carried it off carefully, for he believed the Flopsy Bunnies were still sleeping peacefully inside, but if he had looked behind he would have seen them following at a safe distance!

They watched him go into his house, and then they crept up to the window to listen.

22

Mr McGregor threw down the sack on the stone floor. "One, two, three, four, five, six leetle rabbits!" said Mr McGregor.
(The youngest Flopsy Bunny got upon the window-sill.)

Mrs McGregor took hold of the sack and felt it. She untied the sack and put her hand inside. When she felt the vegetables she became very very angry.

A rotten marrow came flying through the kitchen window, and hit the youngest Flopsy Bunny. It was rather hurt.
  Then Benjamin and Flopsy thought it was time to go home.

What a surprise awaited Mrs Tittlemouse on her return home! When she got back to the parlour, she heard some one coughing in a fat voice, and there sat Mr Jackson! "How do you do, Mr Jackson? Deary me, you have got very wet feet!" said Mrs Tittlemouse. "Thank you, thank you, thank you, thank you, Mrs Tittlemouse! I'll sit awhile and dry myself," said Mr Jackson. He sat and smiled, and the water dripped off his coat tails. Mrs Tittlemouse went round with a mop.

He sat such a while that he had to be asked if he would take some dinner? First she offered him some cherry stones. "No teeth, no teeth, no teeth!" mumbled Mr Jackson, opening his mouth unnecessarily wide; he certainly had not a tooth in his head.

"Thistledown seed, Mr Jackson?" "Tiddly, widdly, widdly! Pouff, pouff, puff!" said Mr Jackson. He blew the thistledown all over the room.

"Thank you, thank you, thank you, Mrs Tittlemouse, but what I really – *really* should like – would be a dish of honey! I can smell it, that's why I came to call." He rose ponderously from the table, and began to look into the cupboards. Mrs Tittlemouse followed with a dish-cloth.

Mr Jackson began to walk down the passage. "Indeed, indeed, you will stick fast, Mr Jackson!" said Mrs Tittlemouse. They went along the sandy passage – "Tiddly widdly –"

"Buzz! Wizz! Wizz!" He met Babbitty round a corner, and snapped her up, and put her down again. "I do not like bumble bees, they are all over bristles," said Mr Jackson, wiping his mouth with his coat sleeve.

"Get out, you nasty old toad!" shrieked Babbitty Bumble. "I shall go distracted!" scolded Mrs Tittlemouse.

Mr Jackson pulled out the bees nest and ate the honey. He seemed to have no objection to stings. The bees gathered up their pollen-bags and flew away, down the passages and out of the windows and doors of the little house, and away over the fields, to find a quieter place for their nest. Mrs Tittlemouse shut herself in the nut cellar.

When Mrs Tittlemouse ventured out of the nut cellar, everybody had gone away. But the untidiness was something dreadful. She went out and fetched some twigs, to partly close up the front door. "I will make it too small for Mr Jackson!"

But she was too tired to do any more. First she fell asleep in her chair, and then she went to bed. "Will it ever be tidy again?" said poor Mrs Tittlemouse.

Next morning she got up very early and did a spring cleaning which lasted a fortnight.

When it was all beautifully neat and clean, she gave a party to five other mice, without Mr Jackson. He smelt the party and came up the bank, but he could not squeeze in at the door. Mrs Tittlemouse had quite forgiven him, and although she had no food to suit his taste, she handed him out acorn-cupfuls of honey-dew through the window, and he was not at all offended.

The flopsy Bunnies did not forget Mrs Tittlemouse.
Next Christmas Thomasina Tittlemouse got a present of
enough rabbit-wool to make herself a cloak and a hood,
and a handsome muff and a pair of warm mittens.

THE END

THE TALE OF
MRS TIGGY-WINKLE
AND
MR JEREMY FISHER

Once upon a time there was a little girl called Lucie, who lived at a farm called Little-town. She was a good little girl — only she was *always* losing her handkerchiefs! "That's three handkins and a pinafore. Oh dear! Have you seen them, Tabby Kitten?"

The kitten went on washing her white paws; so Lucie asked a speckled hen — "Sally Henny-Penny, have *you* found three pocket-handkins?"

But the speckled hen ran away, clucking.

Then Lucie asked Cock Robin. He looked sideways at Lucie with his bright black eye, and flew over a stile and away.

Lucie scrambled up the hill behind Little-town as fast as her stout legs would carry her. "Excuse me sir," Lucie asked Mr Jeremy Fisher, "have you seen my pocket-handkins or even a pinafore?"

"I'm afraid not, young lady," he replied.

Then Lucie saw some pieces of white on the hillside. "They might just be my pocket-handkins," she said.

Presently Lucie came to a spring, bubbling out from the hillside. "Goodness! Who could have put such a tiny bucket there — it's no bigger than an egg-cup! And look at those little foot marks," remarked Lucie. She followed the footprints until she reached a little door in the hillside.

Lucie knocked - once - twice, and a little frightened voice called out "Oh!
Who's that?"

"I'm Lucie. I didn't mean to startle you, but who are you? And have
you seen my pocket handkins?"

"Oh, yes, if you please'm. My name is Mrs Tiggy-winkle. Please do make yourself comfortable," said the little person and she started to iron something.

"What's that?" asked Lucie. "That's not my pocket handkin."

"Oh no," Mrs Tiggy-winkle replied, "that's a little scarlet waistcoat belonging to Cock Robin."

"And, if you please'm, that's a damask tablecloth belonging to Jenny Wren."

"There's one of my pocket handkins," said Lucie, searching through the clothes-basket, "and look, there's my pinny!"

"Fancy that," said Mrs Tiggy-winkle, "they were there all the time. I'll just put the iron over them."

"There!" exclaimed Mrs Tiggy-winkle proudly, holding up Lucie's newly ironed pinny.

"Oh, that *is* lovely!" said Lucie gratefully.

"Goodness, what are they?" asked Lucie pointing to some long yellow things.

"That's a pair of stockings belonging to Sally Henny-penny."

"There's another handkersniff, but it's red," said Lucie.

"That one belongs to Mrs Rabbit and it did so smell of onions, I've had to wash it separately."

"And these are woolly coats belonging to the little lambs at Skelghyl. Now then, I always have to starch these little dicky shirt-fronts. They're Tom Titmouse's and he's most terrible particular."

"I'll just hang these up to air. I'd take it very kindly'm if you would hand the things up to me."

Lucie held up a tattered blue jacket.

"Now there's a story," said Mrs Tiggy-winkle. "Young master Peter Rabbit had a narrow escape from Mr McGregor's garden, but his jacket was left behind, and what with the rain and all . . ."

With all the washing hung up to dry, Mrs Tiggy-winkle and Lucie sat down to take some tea.

Then they tied up all the clothes in bundles and set off to deliver the clean washing.

All the little animals and birds were very much obliged to dear Mrs Tiggy-winkle, and when they came to the bottom of the hill there was nothing left to carry except one little bundle that belonged to Mr Jeremy Fisher.

"I do believe I saw him fishing when I was searching for my handkins," said Lucie as they approached the little house by the pond.

"Ladies, ahoy," greeted Mr Jeremy Fisher.

"I was just about to leave your clean washing and collect from the porch as usual," said Mrs Tiggy-winkle.

"Ah yes, I mean, no, dear lady," said
Mr Jeremy, as Mrs Tiggy-winkle held
up his torn mackintosh. "Little
mishap . . . er, more of an accident . . .
very nearly fatal. Skin of my teeth and
all that!

"A really frightful thing it would
have been, had I not been wearing my
mackintosh — but let me start from
the beginning . . . " and Mr Jeremy
began to tell his story.

The day had started so well for Mr Jeremy Fisher.

"Ah! Nice drop of rain, be good fishing today I shouldn't wonder. I will get some worms and catch a dish of minnows for my dinner. If I catch more than five fish, I will invite my friends Mr Alderman Ptolemy Tortoise and Sir Isaac Newton."

"Now then, my mackintosh, and goloshes. Mmm . . . where did I leave my sandwiches?"

Mr Jeremy Fisher set off with
hops to the place where he kept his
boat.

"I know just the place for minnows,"
he said and pushed the boat into
open water.

He settled himself cross-legged and
arranged his fishing tackle.

The rain trickled down his back and for nearly an hour he stared at the float. "This is getting tiresome. I foresee, I fear, an adjustment to the dinner menu. I will eat a butterfly sandwich and wait till the shower is over."

But then a great water-beetle came
up underneath the lily leaf and
tweaked the toe of one of Mr
Jeremy's galoshes. "You beastly
creature," he complained. Then he
heard a splash from the bank. "I
trust that is not a rat," he said
crossly. "Is there no peace to be had
anywhere?" and he punted off to
find a quieter spot.

Then a little girl asked him if he'd seen her lost handkins.

"I'm afraid not, young lady," he replied. "Dear me, whatever would I be doing with pocket handkins and pinafores, indeed," he chuckled.

But then there was a bobbing of the float and a tugging of the line. "A minnow! A minnow! I have him by the nose! Hooray!"

But Mr Jeremy Fisher got a horrible surprise. He had landed little Jack Sharp, the stickleback.

"Ouch! Jack Sharp – what are you doing on the end of my line? Get off my boat this instant!"

Mr Jeremy sat disconsolately on the edge of his boat worrying about what he would give his guests for dinner.

Then suddenly a *much* worse thing happened. A great big enormous trout came up — ker-pflop-p-p-p! — and seized Mr Jeremy with a snap.

Then it turned and dived down to the bottom of the pond!

But luckily the trout did not like the taste of Mr Jeremy Fisher's mackintosh and spat him out again. He scrambled out on to the nearest bank.

"Never, *never*, have I been so glad to see the light of day," he gasped. "What a mercy it was not a pike! Just look at my best mackintosh — all in tatters."

" . . . And that is what happened," finished Mr Jeremy Fisher. "It was a nightmare, I assure you, truly frightful."

"Oh, mercy me!" exclaimed Mrs Tiggy-winkle anxiously.

"Oh, Miss Lucie," said
Mrs Tiggy-winkle, "here are
Mr Jeremy Fisher's guests. We
must be on our way. I will do
my best with your things sir."

Mr Jeremy and his friends sat down
to dinner. "Perhaps we might take a
glass of pond wine with our roast
grasshopper and ladybird sauce?"

And Mrs Tiggy-winkle hurried home not stopping to give Lucie a bill for the washing.

Lucie watched her as she went and wondered, "But where is your cap and your shawl and your gown? If I didn't know better, Mrs Tiggy-winkle, I would think that you were nothing but a *hedgehog*!"

THE TALE OF
MR TOD

A story about two disagreeable people
called Tommy Brock and Mr Tod

Old Mr Bouncer sat in the spring sunshine outside the burrow, in a muffler, smoking a pipe of rabbit tobacco.

Old Mr Bouncer was stricken in years. He lived with his son Benjamin Bunny and his daughter-in-law Flopsy, who had a young family.

"Now take care of the children Uncle Bouncer," said Flopsy, "we're going out visiting for a while."

The little rabbit-babies were just old enough to open their blue eyes and kick. They lay in a fluffy bed of rabbit wool and hay, in a shallow burrow, separate from the main rabbit hole. To tell the truth – old Mr Bouncer had forgotten them.

Tommy Brock was passing through the woods, with a sack and a little spade which he used for digging, and some mole traps. He was looking for food. Tommy Brock was friendly with old Mr Bouncer; they agreed in disliking Mr Tod.

Old Mr Bouncer sat in the sun, and conversed cordially with Tommy Brock. "What's the news from down hill, Tommy my dear fellow?" said Mr Bouncer. "Not so good I'm sorry to say," said Tommy Brock, "I have not had a good square meal in a fortnight. I shall have to turn vegetarian and eat my own tail!" It was not much of a joke, but old Mr Bouncer laughed.

"My dear old chap, won't you step inside for a slice of seed cake and a glass of homemade cowslip wine to fortify the constitution," he said.

Tommy Brock squeezed himself into the rabbit hole with
alacrity. "Have a cabbage leaf cigar, Tommy, go on,"
said old Mr Bouncer, who was smoking his pipe.
Smoke filled the burrow. Old Mr Bouncer coughed
and laughed; and Tommy Brock puffed and grinned.
   Mr Bouncer laughed and coughed. "I don't get
many visitors, not like it used to be," he
mumbled sleepily. He slumped lower in
his chair and shut his eyes because of
the cabbage smoke . . .

Tommy Brock waited a few moments to be sure that old Mr Bouncer was fast asleep. Then he put all the young rabbit-babies into his sack.

When Flopsy and Benjamin came back – old Mr Bouncer woke up. "Uncle Bouncer, where are the children?" said Flopsy, anxiously. "Father, where are the babies?" asked Benjamin. But Mr Bouncer would not confess that he had admitted anybody into the rabbit hole.

The smell of badger was undeniable, and there were round heavy footmarks in the sand. Mr Bouncer was in disgrace; Flopsy wrung her ears, and slapped him. "It's old Tommy Brock, he's taken our babies," she cried.

"Now don't worry, Flopsy," said Benjamin, "I'll catch that old rogue." Benjamin Bunny set off at once after Tommy Brock.

There was not much difficulty in tracking him; Benjamin soon found his footmarks. He had gone slowly up the winding footpath through the

wood, and his heavy steps showed plainly in the mud.

The path led to a part of the thicket where the trees had been cleared; there were leafy oak stumps, and a sea of blue hyacinths – but the smell that made Benjamin stop, was *not* the smell of flowers!

Mr Tod's stick house was before him and, for once,

Mr Tod was at home. Inside the stick house somebody dropped a plate, and said something. Benjamin stamped his foot, and bolted.

He never stopped until he came to the other side of the wood.

Apparently Tommy Brock had turned the same way. Upon the top of the wall, some ravellings of a sack had caught on a bramble bush.

It was getting late in the afternoon. Other rabbits were coming out to enjoy the evening air. "Cousin Peter! Peter Rabbit, Peter Rabbit!" shouted Benjamin Bunny. "Whatever is the matter, Cousin Benjamin?" asked Peter. "He's bagged my family – Tommy Brock – in a sack, have you seen him?"

Peter had seen Tommy Brock, carrying a sack with "something live in it".

"Cousin Benjamin, compose yourself," he said. "Tommy Brock has gone to Mr Tod's other house at the top of Bull Banks."

And Peter accompanied the afflicted parent, who was all of a twitter. "Hurry Peter; he will be cooking them; come quicker!" said Benjamin Bunny.

Tommy Brock was already in Mr Tod's kitchen, making preparations for supper. (Mr Tod had half a dozen houses, but he was seldom at home. The houses were not always empty when Mr Tod moved *out*; because sometimes Tommy Brock moved *in,* without asking leave).

The sunshine was still warm and slanting on the hill pastures. Half way up, Cotton-tail was sitting in her doorway, with four or five half-grown little rabbits playing about her; one black and the others brown. She had

seen Tommy Brock passing. He had rested nearby a while, pointed to the sack, and seemed doubled up with laughing.

"Squirrel Nutkin, have you seen Tommy Brock?" asked Peter. But he hadn't.

In the wood at Bull Banks, the trees grew amongst heaped up rocks; and there, beneath a crag – Mr Tod had made one of his homes.

The rabbits crept up carefully, listening and peeping. The setting sun made the window panels glow like red flame; but the kitchen fire was not alight. Benjamin sighed with relief. No person was to be seen, and no young rabbits. But the preparations for one person's supper on the table made him shudder.

Then they scrambled round to the other side of the house, and crept up

to the bedroom window. As their eyes became accustomed to the darkness, they perceived that somebody was asleep, lying under a blanket. Tommy Brock's snores came, grunty and regular, from Mr Tod's bed.

They went back to the front of the house, and tried in every way to move the bolt of the kitchen window. They tried to push up a rusty nail between the window sashes; but it was of no use, especially without a light.

In half an hour the moon rose over the wood, and shone full and clear and cold, in at the kitchen window. The light showed a little door beside the kitchen fireplace, belonging to a brick oven. Presently Peter and Benjamin noticed that whenever they shook the window, the little door opposite shook in answer. The young family were alive, shut up in the oven!

They sat side by side outside the window, whispering. There was really not very much comfort in the discovery. Although the young family was alive, the little rabbits were quite incapable of letting themselves out; they were not old enough to crawl.

After much debate, Peter and Benjamin decided to dig a tunnel. "It's the only way. A tunnel right under the house, and into the kitchen." They began to burrow a yard or two lower down the bank. They dug and dug for hours and hours. They could not tunnel straight on account of stones; but by the end of the night they were under the kitchen floor. It was morning – sunrise.

From the fields down below there came the angry
cry of a jay – followed by the sharp yelping bark
of a fox! Then those two rabbits lost their
heads completely. They did the most
foolish thing that they could have
done. They rushed into their short
new tunnel, and hid themselves at
the top end of it, under Mr Tod's
kitchen floor.

Mr Tod was coming up Bull Banks, and
he was in the very worst of tempers.
"Badger . . . Badger . . . I can smell
Badger," he fumed, and slapped his stick
upon the earth; he guessed where Tommy
Brock had gone to.

Mr Tod approached his house very carefully with a large rusty key, and went in. The sight of the table all set out for supper made him furious. But what absorbed Mr Tod's attention was a noise – a deep slow regular snoring grunting noise, coming from his own bed. He peeped around the half-open bedroom door.

Mr Tod came out of the house in a hurry; he scratched up the earth with fury. His whiskers bristled and his coat-collar stood on end with rage. "Badger . . . Badger . . . in my house, in my bed, I'll fix that Badger." He fetched a clothes line and went back into the bedroom.

He stood a minute watching Tommy Brock and listening to the loud snores. Then Mr Tod turned his back towards the bed and undid the window. It creaked; he turned round with a jump. Tommy Brock, who had opened one eye – shut it hastily. The snores continued. Mr Tod pushed the greater part of the clothes line out of the window.

Mr Tod went out at the front door, and round to the back of the house. He took up the coil of line from the window sill, listened for a moment, (Tommy Brock snored conscientiously), and then tied the rope to a tree. "I will wake him with an unpleasant surprise," he said.

Mr Tod fetched a large heavy pailful of water from the spring, and staggered with it through the kitchen into his bedroom. Tommy Brock snored industriously, with rather a snort. He was lying on his back with his mouth open, grinning from ear to ear. One eye was still not perfectly shut.

Then Mr Tod put down the pail, and took up the end of the rope with a hook attached. He gingerly mounted a chair by the head of the bedstead. His legs were dangerously near to Tommy Brock's teeth. He reached up and put the end of rope over the head of the bed, where the curtains ought to hang.

Mr Tod, who was a thin-legged person (though vindictive and sandy whiskered) – was quite unable to lift the heavy weight of the full pail of water to the level of the hook and rope. After much thought he emptied the water into a wash-basin and jug.

The empty pail was not too heavy for him; he slung it up wobbling over the head of Tommy Brock. Surely there never was such a sleeper! Mr Tod got up and down, down and up on the chair.

As he could not lift the whole pailful of water at once, he fetched a milk jug, and ladled quarts of water into the pail by degrees. The pail got fuller and fuller, and swung like a pendulum. Occasionally a drop splashed over; but still Tommy Brock snored regularly and never moved – except one eye.

At last Mr Tod's preparations were complete. "It will make a great mess in my bedroom; but I could never sleep in that bed again without a spring cleaning of some sort," said Mr Tod, and softly left the room. He ran round behind the house, to the tree. He was obliged to gnaw the rope with his teeth – he chewed and gnawed for more then twenty minutes.

The moment he had gone, Tommy Brock got up in a hurry. He peered out of the window and saw Mr Tod

gnawing on the rope.

Tommy Brock rolled Mr Tod's dressing-gown into a bundle, put it into the bed beneath the pail of water instead of himself, and left the room also – grinning immensely. He went into the kitchen, lighted the fire and boiled the kettle; for the moment he did not trouble himself to cook the baby rabbits.

At last the rope snapped. Inside the house there was a great crash and splash.

But no screams. Mr Tod listened attentively. Then he peeped in at the window. In the middle of the bed under the blanket, was a wet flattened *something* – its head was covered by the wet blanket and it was *not snoring any longer*. Mr Tod's eyes glistened. "This has turned out even better than I expected," said Mr Tod. "I will bury that nasty person in a hole. I will have a thorough disinfecting with soap to remove the smell." He hurried round the house to get a shovel . . .

. . . He opened the door . . . Tommy Brock was sitting at Mr Tod's kitchen table, pouring tea from Mr Tod's tea-pot into Mr Tod's tea-cup. He was quite dry, and he was grinning. He threw a cup of scalding tea all over Mr Tod.

Then Mr Tod rushed upon Tommy Brock, and Tommy Brock grappled with Mr Tod amongst the broken crockery, and there was a terrific battle all over the kitchen. To the rabbits underneath, it sounded as if the floor would give way at each crash of falling furniture.

Inside the house the racket was fearful. The rabbit babies in the oven woke up trembling; perhaps it was fortunate they were shut up inside. Everything was broken; the crockery was smashed to atoms. Tommy Brock put his foot in a jar of raspberry jam.

The kettle fell off the hob, and the boiling water out of the kettle fell upon the tail of Mr Tod. Tommy Brock rolled Mr Tod over and over like a log, out at the door.

"Let's get out of here, Benjamin," said Peter. The two rabbits crept out of their tunnel, and hung about amongst the rocks and bushes, listening anxiously.

Tommy Brock and Mr Tod rolled over and over. The snarling and worrying went on, and they rolled over the bank, and down hill, bumping over the rocks. There would never be any love lost between Tommy Brock and Mr Tod.

79

As soon as the coast was clear, Peter Rabbit and Benjamin Bunny came out of the bushes – "Run for it! Run in, Cousin Benjamin! Run in and get them! While I watch the door."

In Mr Tod's kitchen, amongst the wreckage, Benjamin Bunny picked his way to the oven nervously, through a thick cloud of dust. He opened the oven door, felt inside, and found something warm and

wriggling. He lifted it out carefully, and rejoined Peter Rabbit outside.

At home in the rabbit hole, things had not been quite comfortable.

After quarrelling at supper, Flopsy and old Mr Bouncer had passed a sleepless night, and quarrelled again at breakfast.

Old Mr Bouncer could no longer deny that he had invited company into the rabbit hole, but he refused to reply to the questions and reproaches of Flopsy. The day passed heavily.

The two breathless rabbits came scuttering away down Bull Banks, Benjamin half carrying, half dragging a sack, bumpetty bump over the grass. They reached home safely and burst into the rabbit hole.

Great was old Mr Bouncer's relief and Flopsy's joy when Peter and Benjamin arrived in triumph with the young family. "Benjamin, Peter – oh, thank goodness you're all safe," said Flopsy.

"I was a bit worried myself, actually," admitted Mr Bouncer.

Old Mr Bouncer was forgiven. The rabbit-babies were rather tumbled and very hungry; they were fed and put to bed. They soon recovered. Then Peter and Benjamin told their story – but they had not waited long enough to be able to tell the end of the battle between Tommy Brock and Mr Tod.

THE END

THE TALE OF
TWO BAD MICE
AND
JOHNNY TOWN-MOUSE

Once upon a time there was a very beautiful doll's-house; it was red brick with white windows, and it had a front door and a chimney.

It belonged to two dolls called Lucinda and Jane. Jane was the cook; but she never did any cooking, because the dinner had been bought ready-made, in a box full of shavings.

One morning Lucinda and Jane went out for a drive in the doll's perambulator. There was no one in the nursery and it was very quiet.

Presently, there was a little scratching noise in the corner where there was a mouse-hole under the skirting-board. Tom Thumb put out his head. A minute afterwards, Hunca Munca, his wife, put her head out too.

When they saw that there was no one in the nursery, they went cautiously across the hearthrug.

Hunca Munca pushed the front door — it was not locked. "Let's have a look inside" she said.

Tom Thumb and Hunca Munca went upstairs and peeped into the dining-room. Such a lovely dinner was laid out upon the table! There were tin spoons, and lead knives and forks, and two dolly-chairs. "All ready for us!" said Tom Thumb.

Tom Thumb set to work at once to carve the ham, but the knife crumpled up and hurt him; he put his finger in his mouth. "It's not cooked enough. It's hard. You have a try Hunca Munca."

Hunca Munca stood up in her chair, and chopped at the ham with another lead knife. The ham broke off the plate with a jerk, and rolled under the table.

"Let it alone," said Tom Thumb; "give me some fish, Hunca Munca!"

Hunca Munca tried every tin spoon in turn; the fish was glued to the dish.

Then Tom Thumb lost his temper. He put the ham in the middle of the floor, and hit it with the tongs and with the shovel — bang, bang, smash, smash! The ham flew all into pieces. Underneath the shiny paint it was made of nothing but plaster!

"It's no good. You can't eat it!" said Hunca Munca.

Then there was no end to the rage and disappointment of Tom Thumb and Hunca Munca. They broke up the pudding, the lobsters, the pears and the oranges. As the fish would not come off the plate, they put it into the red-hot crinkly paper fire in the kitchen; but it would not burn either.

Tom Thumb went up the chimney and looked out at the top — there was no soot. Hunca Munca found some tiny cans upon the dresser, labelled Rice, Coffee, Sago, but there was nothing inside except red and blue beads.

Then the mice went into the dolls' bedroom. Tom threw Jane's clothes out of the window. Hunca Munca bounced on the bed. After pulling half the feathers out of Lucinda's bolster, she remembered that she herself needed a feather bed. "Let's take this bolster back to our place," she said.

They carried the bolster downstairs and across the hearthrug. "I hope this will be worth all this work," said Tom Thumb. It was difficult to squeeze the bolster into the mouse-hole, but they managed it somehow.

"There. That's lovely!" said Hunca Munca. "Now let's go back and see what else will be useful."

They went back and fetched a chair, a book-case, a bird-cage, and several small odds and ends. The book-case and the bird-cage would not go into the mouse-hole. Hunca Munca left them behind the coal-box, and went to fetch a cradle. "This will be fine for my babies," she said.

Hunca Munca was just returning with another chair, when suddenly there was a noise of talking outside upon the landing. The mice rushed back to their hole, and the dolls came into the nursery.

What a sight met the eyes of Jane and Lucinda!

"What has happened?" asked the little girl who owned the dolls-house.

"It must be mice!" said the nurse.

The book-case and the bird-cage were rescued from under the coal-box — but Hunca Munca has got the cradle, and some of Lucinda's clothes.

She also has some useful pots and pans, and several other things.

The little girl said, "I will get a policeman doll!"

But the nurse said, "I will set a mouse-trap!"

Hunca Munca and Tom Thumb were not the only mice causing trouble that day.

When the cook opened the vegetable hamper, out sprang a terrified Timmy Willie.

"A mouse! A mouse! Call the cat!" screamed the cook.

But Timmy Willie did not wait for the cat. He rushed along the skirting-board till he came to a little hole, and in he popped.

He dropped half a foot, and crashed into the middle of a mouse dinner-party, breaking three glasses.

"Who in the world is this?" inquired Johnny Town-mouse. But after the first exclamation of surprise, he instantly recovered his manners.

He introduced Timmy to nine other mice, all with long tails and white neck-ties. The dinner was of eight courses; not much of anything, but truly elegant. Timmy was very anxious to behave with good manners, but the continual noise upstairs made him so nervous that he dropped a plate.

"Never mind, they don't belong to us," said Johnny. "How did you come here?" he asked.

"I'm from the country," said Timmy Willie. He explained how he had seen the hamper by the garden gate and climbed in. After eating some peas, he had fallen fast asleep. He awoke in a fright, while the

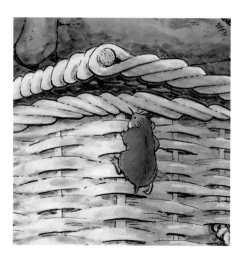

vegetable hamper was lifted into the carrier's cart. Then there was a jolting and a clattering of horses' feet. Timmy Willie trembled amongst the jumbled up vegetables.

At last the cart stopped at a house and the hamper was carried in and set down.

The cook lifted the hamper lid and screamed at the sight of poor Timmy Willie.

"Then I fell in here," finished Timmy.

"And you are most welcome," said Johnny Town-mouse.

Timmy Willie felt quite faint. "Would you like to go to bed?" said
Johnny. "I will show you a most comfortable sofa pillow".

"It is the best bed and I keep it exclusively for visitors," said Johnny Town-mouse. But the sofa smelt of cat. Timmy Willie preferred to spend a miserable night under the fender.

"Oh dear, oh dear!" he sighed. "I wish I was home."

The next day things were no better for Timmy Willie. He could not eat the food, and the noise prevented him from sleeping. In a few days he grew so thin that Johnny Town-mouse questioned him. "Are you ill?"

"Oh no," replied Timmy, "but I do so miss my peaceful sunny bank and my friend, Cock Robin."

"Well," said Johnny Town-mouse, "it may be that your teeth and digestion are unaccustomed to our food. Perhaps it might be wiser for you to return the way you came — in the hamper, to your own home in the country."

"Oh? Oh!" cried Timmy.

"Why of course. Did you not know that the hamper goes back empty on Saturdays?" said Johnny, rather huffily.

So Timmy Willie said goodbye to his new friends and hid in the hamper with a crumb of cake.

After much jolting, he was set down safely in his own garden.

"How good to be back!" said Timmy, in delight.

Sometimes on Saturdays he went to look at the hamper lying by the gate, but he knew better than to get in again. And nobody got out, though Johnny Town-mouse had half promised a visit.

*

Timmy Willie slept through the winter and the sun came out again in Spring.

Timmy Willie had nearly forgotten his visit to the town, when up the sandy path all spick and span with a brown leather bag came Johnny Town-mouse!

Timmy Willie received him with open arms. "You have come at the best of times. We will have herb pudding and sit in the sun."

"Hmm! It is a little damp" said Johnny Town-mouse.

"How are Tom Thumb and all our friends?" asked Timmy.

Johnny explained that the family had gone to the seaside. The cook was doing spring cleaning, with particular instructions to clear out the mice. There were four kittens and the cat had killed the canary.

"Tom Thumb has told the small mice all about the trap, and Hunca Munca has become quite good friends with the policeman-doll, although he never says anything, and always looks quite stern," said Johnny.

"What is that fearful noise?" asked Johnny Town-mouse.

"Oh, that's only a cow." said Timmy. "I will go and beg a little milk."

They were just setting off down the path, when Cock Robin flew down.

"Hide!" shouted Johnny, in fright.

"It's only my friend Cock Robin saying hello. Come along, Johnny, we haven't got all day."

"Whatever is that fearful racket?" said Johnny Town-mouse.

"That's only the lawn-mower," said Timmy. "Now we can fetch some fresh grass clippings to make up your bed."

Johnny waited while Timmy went to fetch the milk and the fresh grass. When he returned, it began to rain. "Oh! My tail is getting all wet!" complained Johnny.

"It's only a spring shower. Here, take this leaf and hold it over your head like this," said Timmy. "The rain will brighten up the flowers. Come along, Johnny."

"I am sure you will never want to live in town again," said Timmy Willie to Johnny Town-mouse.

But he did! He went back in the very next hamper of vegetables. He said it was too quiet.

Johnny got back safely to his town-house and his old friends.

As for the two bad mice, they were
not so very naughty after all, because
Tom Thumb paid for everything he
broke. He found a crooked sixpence
under the hearthrug; and upon
Christmas Eve, he and Hunca Munca
stuffed it into one of the stockings of
Lucinda and Jane.

  And very early every morning,
Hunca Munca comes with her
dustpan and broom to sweep the
dollies' house!

But Timmy Willie stayed in the country and he never went to town again. One place suits one person, another place suits another person. For my part I prefer to live in the country, like Timmy Willie.